THE STATION CAT

STEPHEN HOGTUN

A STORY OF KINDNESS AND HOPE

The colour had drained from this place a long time ago.

A cold, damp railway station and a platform forlorn,
Peeling black paint on wrought iron benches,
Passengers and travellers without light, in drab, formal lines,
Dull brass railings, covered in grime from a thousand passing hands.

Soot covered chimney pots where smoke-coloured jackdaws squawked,
Chipped wooden herringbone floors made ashen with dirt
and worn from the trudge of heavy footsteps shuffling along.

Spiked fences, smoked glass, shrill whistles, hissed steam
and muted whispers, all burnt upon the passing breeze.
An oversized station clock hung heavy from its aging bracket.
Its ticking and tocking sullen, as all passed under its unforgiving and watchful gaze.

In this place, sadness resides,
For no one knows where all the colour hides.

Through a gap in the fence a small cat appeared,
Wearing scrapes and tears.
She was skinny and weak with twisted tail
and she called for her mother along the steel train tracks.

Her cries went ignored and unanswered,
and glancing, cold looks returned to ink-stained broadsheets.

She climbed onto the platform along the broken, stone brickwork
and shuffled around the legs of waiting passengers,
Bumping her head in hope for affection.
A short, brutal life without warmth
and invisible to stern faces turning away.

If they had only looked closer they would have seen...

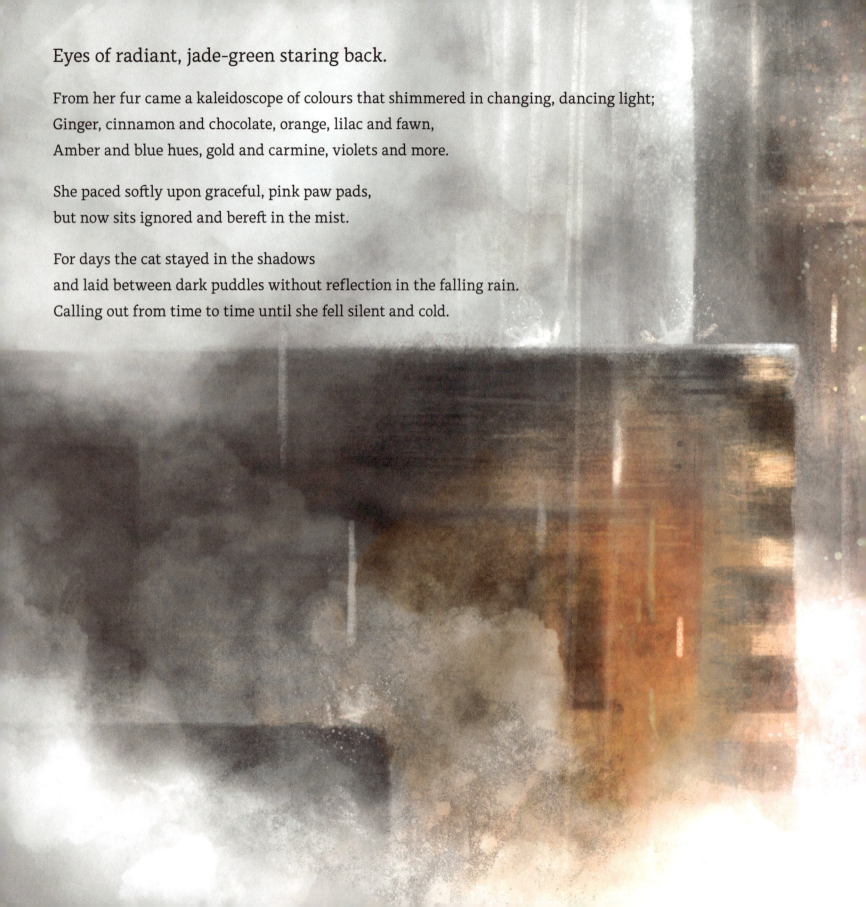

Eyes of radiant, jade-green staring back.

From her fur came a kaleidoscope of colours that shimmered in changing, dancing light;
Ginger, cinnamon and chocolate, orange, lilac and fawn,
Amber and blue hues, gold and carmine, violets and more.

She paced softly upon graceful, pink paw pads,
but now sits ignored and bereft in the mist.

For days the cat stayed in the shadows
and laid between dark puddles without reflection in the falling rain.
Calling out from time to time until she fell silent and cold.

Amongst the coming and going of trains,
The station stayed sombre and lifeless
and the familiar ding of the crossing bell sounded.
People looked up as the announcement came out,

*"The train now approaching Platform One...
Is the Fourteen Twenty-Two to Wivelsfield."*

From a cloud of billowing steam it appeared,
Gliding in silence and vapour,
A pale train void of any colour at all.
Its carriage door opened and a conductor with kindly eyes looked out,

He studied his passenger list but there were no names to call this time.

Before the train departed the cat emerged from the shadows and walked
    towards it.
A train to take her away, anywhere from here,
and she stood weakly and let out a fearful sound.

The conductor looked down at the weary cat,
A spectrum of colours set against the
　　background of the dark and the white,
and shook his head gently.

"This train is not for you,
and you have no ticket,
You will have to save to come aboard.
I'll see you again,
but don't be down, young kitten."

He waved his white flag and steam appeared.
The train disappeared into the clouds without a single sound being heard.

And the train came and went.

The cat went back to the darkness,
Searching for a home, a place that went unfound,
and watched from its hidden spot all come and go.
Crowds of people went about their sorrow without noticing her at all.

She watched a wistful man in a bowler hat sit each early morning
Before he sighed and got on the same train.
The sighs became heavier with every passing day.
Black umbrella under-arm, trench coat, starched collar,
Sagging shoulders and broken expression.

The wistful man finished one of his plain sandwiches from wax paper
and his head dropped forward.
He glanced at the train tracks that would take him away.

The cat approached and twirled
between his legs as he sat.
"A runaway, are you?" the man said,
"Looking for your place in...?"
But his words drifted off.

The cat jumped up into his lap,

So the man stroked her shimmering fur
and they sat in near silence,
Except for the quiet whisper of her purr.

*"I wanted to be a painter when I was younger
but I had mouths to feed.*

So I go to the city early and come home late."
The cat curled up tight in his lap.

*"But they grew up and I wasn't around half as
much as I could have...*

As I should have.... ."

He looked at the cat's colour glistening in the light
and something forgotten became memory again.
His eyes welled up and, as he wiped away the tears, colour returned to his face.

The wistful man's train approached the platform
    but when he went to stand, he found that he couldn't.

The cat was small but, in that moment, weighed so heavy.

The man carried on stroking her fur
smiling and laughing,
With visions and thoughts of fulfilling a dream.
He didn't board with the other passengers and remained.

And the train came and went.

The cat continued living on the platform and watched all
    come and go.

She had noticed a faded schoolboy arrive each day.
He hung back from the crowd of other children,
Dark circles under his eyes, torn uniform, frayed laces
Tear-burnt cheeks and vacant gaze.

He had caught the train heading north each day
but today he looked to the gap in the fence
and to the dark woods it concealed.

The faded boy turned and nervously paced towards it.

He went to walk through the gap but he found that he couldn't.
The cat had run towards him from the shadows
and she pulled and pulled at his trousers.

The cat was small but, in that moment,
    became so strong.

The boy sank down onto the platform floor
and the cat approached and brushed her head against him.
He ran his hand through her colourful fur.
"I'm so alone," cried the boy
and they sat in near silence,
Except for the quiet whisper of her purr.

"You're here all alone too," said the boy,
"Don't you get lonely?"
The cat began to clean and paw at his hand.

"Will you be here when I get back from school?"
    the faded boy asked,
"I never have anyone to greet me."

He looked at the cat's colour
and something taken was returned again.

His cheeks went red and flush with cheer.

The boy stroked the cat goodbye and boarded
   with the other school children, smiling
and telling them what he had seen.

And the train came and went.

The cat grew stronger and found her place at the station.
She would keep mice at bay and greet the boy every day
and the wistful man would bring food whenever he could.

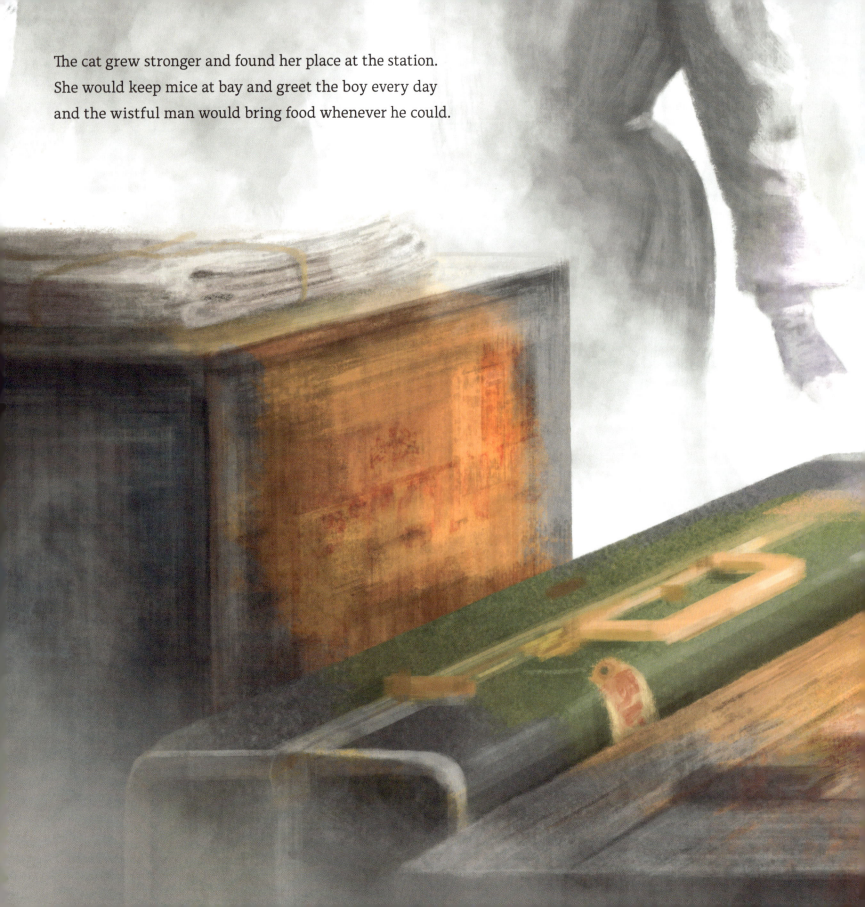

The cat had noticed the saddest person of all,
A woman dressed in black who would weep each day.

She would arrive with white lilies and return with flowers wilted and dried.
Veiled face, ruffled dress, muddied shoes.
Tears and petals would fall where she stood
and no matter how many of either fell there always seemed to be more.

The woman floated through the crowd
murmuring words about grace.
On her arm hung charms of gold hearts on a fragile bracelet.

Each day she caught the train to the valley and returned at suppertime.
One day the cat noticed something was different.
The woman laid the flowers on the station bench
and headed towards the coast train travelling the other way,
To lost beaches and crumbling white cliffs.

As the woman went to board the train, she found that she couldn't.
The cat had run towards her from the darkness
and she blocked the door so the woman could not pass.

The cat was small but, in that moment, she appeared so large.

The woman dressed in black slumped back on the bench
 next to the lilies and sobbed.
The cat twisted around her before settling on her lap.
"You look like a beautiful bouquet," the woman said
While she stroked her glistening fur
and they sat in near silence,
Except for the quiet whisper of her purr.

"All the best flowers are picked first," she said as she looked at her lilies
"Why do all the pretty things last the least?"
and with that she let out all the pain she had held for years.
The cat stood up and bumped her head against hers.
She stared back at the cat's colour
as the cat played with the charms on her bracelet.

The woman dressed in black let out a laugh
and something once heard was echoed again.

She stroked the cat before drying her eyes
and picked up her white lilies before standing.
The woman got on her usual train to the valley that she took each day
With flowers to her chest, and smile returned,
Her lips turned to colour as she held them.

And the train came and went.

The cat grew older and happy and was stroked by all who waited.

People would miss trains to talk to her and keep her company,
Children would endlessly play with her and her bowl was never left empty.

The cat lived a long, happy life full of company and love,
An endless stream of petting and warmth
and with old age her fur turned grey and the platform seemed to bloom.

The colour had returned to this place a long time ago.

A warm, pleasant railway station and a platform bright,
Freshly painted vivid shades on cushioned benches,
Passengers and travellers without cares, in happy conversation, scattered about.
Polished golden brass railings made gleaming by hand,
Heated chimney pots where brightly coloured songbirds danced and sang,
Waxed wooden herringbone floors reflecting the light blue sky
which chorused the light footsteps that now skipped along it.

Welcome signs, glistening glass, kind greetings, warm handshakes
and gentle laughter, all carried on the passing breeze.
An oversized station clock watching over anew,
Its ticking and tocking a caring beat and rhythm to the movement below.

In this place happiness resides,
For everyone knows this is where the colour thrives.

The man once wistful hung his paintings from
    the station for all to admire.

Paintings of freedom and carefree brushstrokes,

That seemed to shimmer and glimmer

in changing, dancing lights.

The boy once faded had grown up strong and bright.

He had been made Station Master and kept all gleaming.

He made everyone welcome with smiles,

Smart trousers and polished shoes,

with rosy cheeks and bold stride.

The woman once dressed in black had lovingly
    planted flowers and hanging baskets
That exploded with new life for all to see.
Primroses, pink Fuchsias and Impatiens,
Sweet Peas, Snap Dragons and Campanulas
and graceful, flowing Forget-Me-Nots.

Everyone talked and laughed and smiled,
and in the middle, our station cat, old and grey,
Tired, yet content and restful.
She watched as all about continued, unburdened.

Then came the familiar ding of the crossing bell
and the call came out,

*"The train now approaching Platform One...
Is the Fourteen Twenty-Two to Wivelsfield."*

But the crowd didn't notice as they talked and bustled and played.
From a cloud of billowing steam it appeared,
Gliding in silence and vapour,
A pale train void of any colour at all.

Its carriage door opened and the conductor with kindly eyes looked out.
He glanced at his passenger list and there was but one name to call.
The cat looked up knowingly
and hobbled forwards
Towards the train
A carriage to take her away, her journey over.

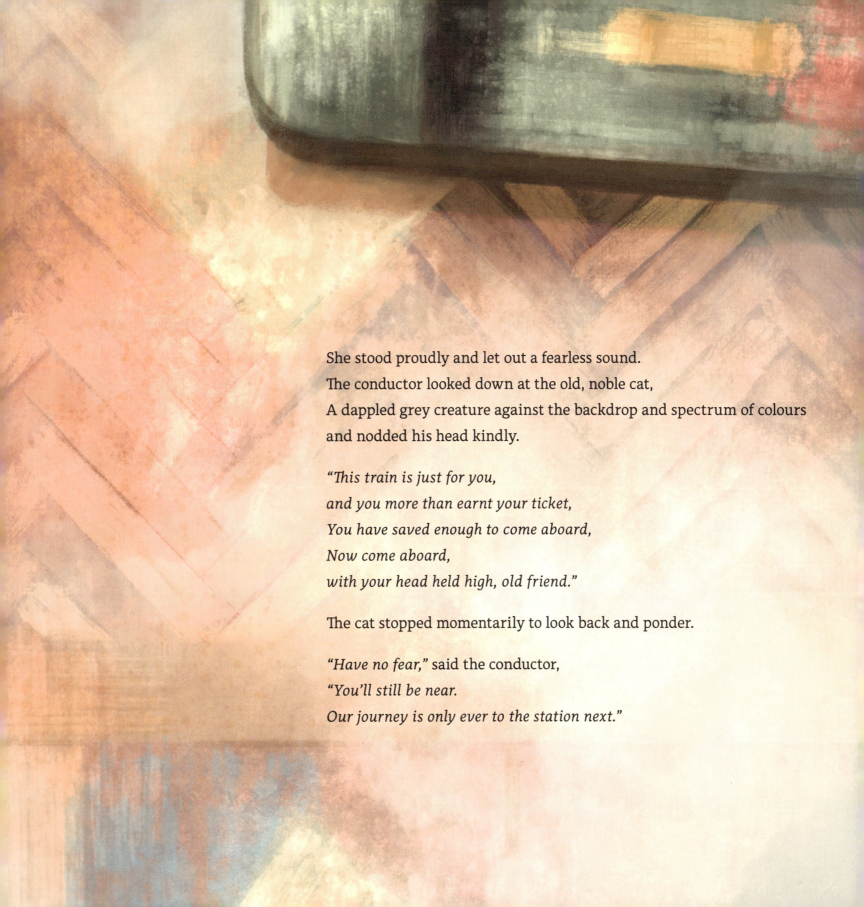

She stood proudly and let out a fearless sound.
The conductor looked down at the old, noble cat,
A dappled grey creature against the backdrop and spectrum of colours
and nodded his head kindly.

"This train is just for you,
and you more than earnt your ticket,
You have saved enough to come aboard,
Now come aboard,
with your head held high, old friend."

The cat stopped momentarily to look back and ponder.

"Have no fear," said the conductor,
"You'll still be near.
Our journey is only ever to the station next."

The cat got on

and the conductor waved his white flag and steam appeared.

The train disappeared into the clouds without a single noise being heard,

Except for the quiet whisper of her purr,

And the train came and went.

STEPHEN HOGTUN

Stephen Hogtun is an author and illustrator who lives on the west coast of Norway with his partner, two children, and many rescue animals.

Their house is an old stone building which they completely rebuilt by hand, on a beautiful spot overlooking a fjord. On their first day there, amongst the crumbling stone work, overgrown garden, and leaking roof, a lost cat appeared from the forest. The cat promptly walked into the house and decided this is where she would now live.

They named her Georgie.

Despite the challenges they faced building the house on their own, and struggling with all the problems they encountered, Georgie was always there to bring colour and happiness to the situation with her love and kindness. She made the house a home.

This book is inspired by her and dedicated to her memory.

Written and illustrated by Stephen Hogtun
Created and designed for DK by Plum5 Ltd

Managing Editor Laura Gilbert
Project Editor Robin Moul
Senior Art Editor Rachael Parfitt Hunt
Production Editor Abi Maxwell
Senior Production Controller Inderjit Bhullar
Jacket Co-ordinator Issy Walsh
Deputy Art Director Mabel Chan
Publisher Francesca Young
Publishing Director Sarah Larter

First published in Great Britain in 2022 by
Dorling Kindersley Limited
DK, One Embassy Gardens, 8 Viaduct Gardens,
London, SW11 7BW

The authorised representative in the EEA is
Dorling Kindersley Verlag GmbH. Arnulfstr. 124,
80636 Munich, Germany

Text copyright © Stephen Hogtun 2022
Layout and design © 2022 Dorling Kindersley Limited
A Penguin Random House Company
10 9 8 7 6 5 4 3 2 1
001–323176–April/2022

A CIP catalogue record for this book
is available from the British Library.
ISBN: 978-0-2414-8809-6

Printed and bound in Latvia

For the curious
www.dk.com